Mamaw's
TENETS
FOR LIFE

20 Principles
for Living a Great Life

KEITH A. CRAFT

Printed in the United States of America.

First printing edition 2019.

ISBN: 978-1-7330945-0-4 (Paperback)

1% Publishing
8500 Teel Parkway
Frisco, TX 75034

(214)387-9833

Dedication

I want to dedicate this book to my wife, Sheila. I found you when we were 15. I have come to realize two things that I am most grateful for:

> First, I did not know at 15, that I was looking for someone who carried the same sweetness of spirit that my Mamaw carried. But through the years, as I have reflected about how God brought us together so early, I've realized that's exactly what my early connect with you was... your sweetness. Little did I know, that my hero, Mamaw, would create a desire in me for a SHERO like you.

> Second, the Bible says, *"The man who finds a wife finds a treasure, and he receives favor from the Lord."* [Proverbs 18:22 NLT]

I will be forever grateful to God for the favor He has given me, because of YOU!

I will forever be grateful for my Mamaw who gave me a picture of what sweetness looked like, so I knew who to search for and find... a treasure... like YOU!

There is no one like YOU, Sheila. You are the best of best friends.

You are the greatest treasure I have ever found.

You are the sweetest wife, mother, and grandmother EVER.

And for all those reasons and more... I call you... PRECIOUS.

Our family of choice, Elevate Life Church, calls you Pastor Precious.

And maybe the most beautiful thing of all... our grandchildren only know you as... PRECIOUS.

Thank YOU for being our PRECIOUS!

Contents

Introduction

The fondest memories of my childhood are the times I got to spend in the presence of my Grandma (Mamaw). When I was growing up, I had no way of knowing that I was receiving daily principles from a live-in life coach...long before there was such a thing. Every day she would speak life principles into me that were making me a better me, by the way she lived, loved, and caringly directed...without me even knowing it. She lived what she said, and she said what she lived.

The thing I remember most about her was her sweetness. To me, she was the personification of love wrapped in flesh. One of the reasons I felt this way was because of the way she not only made me feel in her presence, but also the way she made me feel about me. She always called me special names like "honey, baby, and sweetie" to name a few. The way she smiled, you could hear her smile in her voice. The way she spoke with lovingkindness. The way she touched, it all said, "I love you so much." From the time I was a small boy, as I would approach her, she would intentionally touch my face and my nose. She made me feel like I was the most loved person on the planet.

I did not know to call her a life coach, but when I look back on my life, that is what she was. I knew she was the one person that knew me and wanted the best for me. She was masterful in the way that she would create an expectation and lovingly inspire me to not just to live up to the expectation, but make me want to pursue excellence. She would lay out what she expected and then she would inspect it. And what she did in between the "expect and inspect" is not only deeply imbedded in my heart and soul, but has helped me to help many people in their personal and professional life do the same. You will discover that simple yet profound process in this book.

Warren Buffett said, "When you find someone you admire, do the same things they did that you admire, and you will become admirable."

That is what I have attempted to do in my life and through this book. The following "tenets" are the principles that I personally witnessed my Mamaw living out in her everyday life. My hope is that in reading this book, you will not only be inspired to live by my Mamaw's Tenets for Life, but you will inspire others to do the same like... she did for me and maybe like her to me, you will become someone's HERO... a person who is admired or idealized for courage, outstanding achievements or notable qualities.

Chapter 1

The Malibu Adventures

Are you guys ready? We need to leave soon," Mamaw said as she headed towards to the front door. "We don't want to be late to church."

Ray, Allen, and their sister Cindy followed close behind. "I call the front seat," said Ray as everyone crawled into the 1964 blue four door Chevrolet Malibu.

The ride to church with Mamaw was always adventurous. From the very beginning when he had taught her to drive, her son-in-law, Monroe, said, "We are going to make sure and put as much steel around you as we can to protect you and my children when they are riding with you."

"Watch out Mamaw!" Ray shouted, as she almost hit the car in front of her because the light turned red. "Whew! That was close Mamaw." Ray said.

Mamaw had a big smile on her face like she always did, and even when Ray yelled out, she stayed calm. "God has got us. He always has and always will, but thank you for warning me!"

The church service was both compelling and convicting. At the end of the pastor's message, Allen turned to Mamaw and said, "I want to go up to the altar and pray."

"Me too. Let's go together." Mamaw whispered. She reached over and gently took Allen by the hand. Immediately he felt love in her touch. Her hands were always so soft… so tender… so embracing.

"What is it about her holding my hand that makes me feel so loved ?" Allen wondered as a tear from his left eye began to stream down his face. They walked down the aisle together and knelt at the altar.

"Heavenly Father, thank You for my grandson Allen. Thank you that he has a heart for You. I ask that You would put your hand on his life and use him for Your purpose." With that, Mamaw drew close to Allen and wrapped her loving arms around him. In the background there was a song being sung by everyone, "*He touched me…oh He touched me. And oh, the joy that floods my soul. Something happened and now I know, He touched me and made me whole.*"

One of our favorite things to do after church was to go to lunch at El Papas. It wasn't traditional Mexican food, but Tex/Mex, Mexican food with a Texas flair. Everyone loved the chips, salsa, and queso, all served before the meal. Ray always had the Enchilada Dinner: two enchiladas with rice and beans. Allen liked the Megalito Plate, with enchiladas and a taco.

On the way to the restaurant, Mamaw said with her usual, beautiful smile, "It was a very special service today. I really felt God's presence. I remember a story about Abraham Lincoln." As she began to speak in her sweet-sounding voice, a car slammed on its breaks and began to honk its horn. A man yelled out as he sped by, "Watch where you are going lady! I almost hit you!"

Cindy asked, "What happened? Why is he so angry?"

"I'm not sure," Mamaw said calmly with her usual big smile on her face.

Then Ray spoke up and said, "Mamaw, I think there was a stop sign back there and you didn't stop!"

Mamaw replied, "One thing is for sure, God has got us! He always has and He always will, but thank you for telling me about the stop sign Ray. I'll be more aware next time."

Allen said, "Mamaw tell us the Abraham Lincoln story. I love stories about Abraham Lincoln! Did you know he was 6'4" Mamaw?"

"Yes, I did Allen, and I think you just may be tall like him!"

"I hope you're right Mamaw! Tell us the story," Allen urged.

Mamaw began… "As President of the United States, he would visit different churches week in and week out in the Washington D.C. area. One day after church," Mamaw continued as she was driving, "a reporter asked President Lincoln how church was today. He said, *'You know, the message was wonderful, but the preacher fell short, I felt, because he did not give people the opportunity to respond to the message. I just believe everyone needs a chance to respond to God, and it would do all mankind some good to spend time at the altar.'*"

As she pulled the blue Malibu into the driveway, Mamaw said, "That's what we did today Allen. We responded to God…. We spent some time at the altar and that's why we can always know…" Mamaw put the Malibu in park, turned off the key, and turned around and said, "God's got us. He always has and always will, and for that, we will always be thankful."

Tenet #1

God's got us. He always has and He always will, and for that, we will always be thankful.

Chapter 2

Get To

As Mamaw opened the door to get out of the car, she let out a groan. "What's wrong Mamaw?" Allen asked.

"It's my left arm honey. It just hurts sometimes. That's all," she said with a smile on her face.

"What happened... why does it hurt?" Cindy asked.

Mamaw gave the front door key to Allen and said, "Do you mind unlocking the front door for us baby?"

"Sure Mamaw!"

"What happened to your arm Mamaw?" Cindy asked again as they walked into the house.

"I'll tell you about it later sweetheart. Right now I'm going to lay down and take a nap. That's one of my favorite things about Sunday! We GET TO go to church. We GET TO eat Mexican food! We GET TO be together! We GET TO take a nap! We GET TO enjoy this day that the Lord has made. We GET TO be glad in it!"

Mamaw continued, "I have discovered that my life is happier when I realize that I GET TO rather than HAVE TO. We always need to realize that every day we live is a GET TO not a HAVE TO. You see, when we understand that God made everything for us... the trees, the grass, the ocean, every sunset and every sunrise He made for us. Everything He created that was created, He created for us to enjoy and BE glad! God created the earth not just to be a dwelling place for man, but to be a visual picture of what heaven is like on the earth."

Ray, Allen, and Cindy stood speechless in the living room as Mamaw spoke. She had been a Sunday School teacher for over 40 years.

"That's what Sunday is all about. The book of Genesis tells the story:

'So, the creation of the heavens and the earth and everything in them was completed. On the seventh day God had finished the work of creation, so he rested from all his work. And God blessed the seventh day and declared it holy, because it was the day when he rested from all his work of creation.'

I GET TO rest today and I am going to go lay down right now!"

"Well" said Cindy, "I am going to GET TO go play!"

Allen looked at Ray and asked, "You want to play a game of horse with me?"

"Yes! I can't wait to GET TO beat you!"

"Mamaw, while you GET TO take a nap, we GET TO play! I love Sundays!" Allen exclaimed.

Tenet #2

Every day we live is a GET TO, not a
HAVE TO.

Chapter 3

Sunday Funday

Ray and Allen changed clothes to go outside and play their game of horse. They walked hurriedly down the hall, stopping briefly in the kitchen to get some water from the icebox. "Ok," Ray said, "We will shoot to see who goes first."

"Alright! Then I will take the first shot to see who goes first!" Allen said.

About that time, Mamaw walked into the kitchen. "No, I will shoot first to see who will be first!" Ray said. "I am the oldest and that means I will go first to see who shoots first." The boys walked into the den and stopped at the sliding glass door to unlock it. Mamaw listened as the argument continued.

"Just because you are the oldest, doesn't mean you GET TO be first! I called it and I am going first!" Allen said sternly. "Mamaw, who should go first to see who shoots first in our game of horse?" Allen asked.

"Well, I guess you need to decide who wants to be last," Mamaw answered.

"What do you mean Mamaw?" Ray asked.

"Why do you think it's important to be first?" Mamaw asked.

"I don't know" said Ray. "I just think I should go first because I am the oldest."

Allen retorted, "But I called it, Mamaw!"

"There is something in all of us that wants to go first. Maybe we all think that it's important to be first because we think going first and being first make us important." Mamaw continued, "Jesus dealt with this all the time. On one occasion, His disciples came to Him and asked, 'Who is going to be the greatest?' Jesus said, 'the one who serves the other is the greatest.'

Another time a rich man asks Him, 'I have a lot of money, but how do I GET TO have eternal life?' Jesus answered, 'Go sell all your possessions and give the money to the poor and you will have what is most important, riches in heaven. Then come and follow me.' But the young rich man couldn't do it. No, he wouldn't do it, because his money was more important to him than anything. Jesus went on to say to him, 'But many who are the greatest now, will be least important then. . . .'"

"But Mamaw, we are just talking about a game of horse and who is going to go first," Allen said.

Mamaw smiled and walked over to where the boys were standing at the sliding glass door. "Look out there. It's Sunday Funday! See that trampoline? Whether it's jumping on that, or playing your game of horse, God made it all for you to enjoy! So, to have fun in life, you can't worry about who is going to be first," she said as she put both boy's faces into her gentle

Mamaw's Tenets for Life

hands. "Let's remember 'This is the day the Lord has made,' for us. That makes each of us important to God. But who goes first to see who shoots first in your game of horse is not what is most important. The most important thing to remember for a Sunday FUNDAY is that the one who chooses to be last, is the one who chooses to be the greatest."

"Huh?" said Allen.

"Yes." said Mamaw. "The greatest... the most important people are the ones who put others before themselves, and in doing so you are serving their best interests above your own. And that's why Jesus said, 'I came to serve, not to be served, and the first shall be last and the last shall be first.' So, the question is not who is going to go first to see who will shoot first, it's who wants to be last?"

Allen quickly spoke up and said, "You go first Ray!"

And Ray said, "Did I not already call first?"

"Give me a hug. I'm going to take my Sunday Funday nap!" Mamaw said. "Hey, you boys never got that water. Go ahead and go outside. I'll bring it to you."

Tenet #3

The most important people are the ones who put others before themselves, and in doing so, you are serving their best interests above your own.

Chapter 4

After Church

Part of the Sunday Funday was Sunday night After Church. This was always a time when all the cousins, Aunts, and Uncles would go to one of the families' houses after church.

Immediately following church, Mamaw and the children walked across the church parking lot towards the car. It always took what seemed like an eternity to GET TO the car. No matter the time of day on Sunday, every person in the parking lot always wanted to talk to Mamaw. It seemed as if everyone wanted to be in her presence.

"Hello Mamaw. How are you doing?" Mrs. Ingram asked.

"Oh, honey I'm doing just fine. But the question is how are you doing? How's Kelly doing?" Mamaw reached out and took her hand. Mrs. Ingram's daughter Kelly had just had surgery.

"She's getting better, but it was worse than the doctors thought, and her recovery is going to take several months rather than weeks."

"I am so sorry to hear that. Let's pray right now. Allen, come over here and pray for Kelly; we know God's got us.

He always has and He always will."

Ray and Cindy walked to the car and patiently waited. They knew Mamaw was putting Mrs. Ingram first like she did everyone she ever came across.

Finally in the car, "Whose house are we going to tonight Mamaw?" Cindy asked.

"Your Uncle David and Aunt Pat's house." Mamaw answered.

"I love to go to their house!" Allen said. "They have the most fun things to do! I love Sunday Funday!"

It was about a thirty-minute drive and so Allen said, "Mamaw, you never told us what happened to your arm?"

"Well honey, it's a long story and since we have a little time that we GET TO spend together, I will tell you as much as I can.

In 1956, I begin to feel some pain in my chest and so your mother took me to the doctor. We were there for a while, in fact it seemed like forever...."

As she was talking Allen asked, "Mamaw, can I roll down the window?"

"Yes," Mamaw said. The sun was beginning to set, and as Allen rolled down the window, he smelled the fresh air as the wind began to beat against his face. After talking to Mamaw earlier in the day, he noticed the trees more. He noticed how green the grass was. As he looked into the beautiful sunset, he thought, "Thank You God. You made this all for me." Allen had never noticed the beauty of everything around him before as he did in that moment. "The fresh air... the trees, the grass, the sky, the sun... all just for me to enjoy."

Mamaw continued, "The doctor finally came into the room where your mother and I had been waiting and said, "There is no easy was to say this, but you have breast cancer."

"You had cancer Mamaw?" Cindy gasped.

"Yes, I did sweetie. That day we found out that I would need a mastectomy."

"What is a mastectomy Mamaw?" Allen asked.

Ray answered solemnly, "It means her breasts had to be removed."

Everyone in the blue Malibu was quiet—

"Yes, darlings, that's what it meant." Mamaw said.

"But what does that have to do with your arm hurting Mamaw?" questioned Allen.

"Well honey, when they removed my breast, they recommended a new laser type of radiation treatment. My cancer was very serious, so they wanted to make sure they not only got all of it, but that it didn't spread."

"So, what happened to your arm?" Cindy asked. "Why does it hurt?"

"After the radiation treatments, my body was severely burned on the outside. It has been more than 20 years and I still struggle," Mamaw replied.

"Are we almost there Mamaw?" Cindy asked.

"Yes baby, it will be just a few minutes more."

"Finish telling us Mamaw," Allen said, "about your arm."

"Anyway, my left arm has never been the same. It stays swollen and sometimes I can barely use it. And today, it was really bothering me."

Ray asked, "Shouldn't those doctors be held responsible

17

After Church

for what happened to you Mamaw? That's so awful that 20 years later you are still struggling. Doesn't it make you angry? It makes me angry."

"Yeah me too Mamaw." Allen said. "It makes me sad... sad for you."

"When I heard 'you have cancer,' it was so difficult, and yet I remember immediately saying to your mom, 'God's got us. He always has and He always will.' The doctors told us that this new laser radiation treatment was new and radical. They explained that it could kill me. So I went into it knowing that it was untried and dangerous, but I was willing to take the risk because I wanted to live. Now 20 years later," she said with a smile on her face, "here I am, and you know what the best part is?"

"What Mamaw? What's the best part?" asked Allen.

Mamaw paused for a moment and said, "I GET TO be with you on the Sunday Funday! And I want you to know I have realized something very important over the last 20 years of dealing with this struggle."

"What is that Mamaw?" Ray asked.

"I've realized that you cannot dictate everything that happens to you, but you can dictate what happens in you. And what's happened inside me is that I want to be more loving to the people in my life. I want to be grateful for each day I have to live. I want to enjoy every second of everyday and I want to spend as much time as I can with all of you!!! Well, here we are! Let's go inside and have the best Sunday Funday EVER!"

Tenet #4

You cannot dictate everything that happens TO you, but you can dictate what happens IN you.

Chapter 5

Wake Up to Make Up

Monday mornings always came too fast and too early. Ray and Allen were asleep in their bunkbeds when they both heard Mamaw joyfully say, "Rise and shine boys! This is the day that the Lord has made, let us rejoice and be glad in it!"

Allen said, "Is it already Monday morning?"

"Yes, it is honey," Mamaw said, "so let's get up and get ready for school. Be sure and make up your beds and after you get dressed come help me fix breakfast."

"Mamaw, can I ask you something?" Allen said in a tired voice. "Why do we have to make up our beds every day?"

"Yeah," Ray joined in, "What's the big deal with that? I was talking to one of my friends the other day and asked him if he had to make up his bed every day? He told me 'No' and said, 'Why would you make up your bed when you just going to mess it up that same night?'"

As the boys sat on the edge of their bunkbeds trying to wake up, Mamaw stepped toward them and said, "It's not about making up your bed, it's about leaving things undone. It's not about sheets and covers or pillows. It's about taking pride in your space." She paused and looked into both of their eyes and said, "Making up your bed is not as much about doing a task or even just completing a task, but it is about being your best. Making up your bed... think about that boys... we don't make down our bed, we make UP our bed! Why? Because we are going UP in life! And to GO UP in life, you have to learn that you can MAKE things GO UP!

So, say to yourself, 'This bed is messed up. In fact, I am the one that messed it up. And if I messed it up, I can MAKE IT UP!' By choosing to Wake up and MAKE UP your bed, you're learning to wake up to what you can make GO UP."

"Well right now I'm going to jump down from this top bunk," Ray said with a chuckle, "because I have to go to the bathroom!"

As Allen stood up from the bottom bunk, Mamaw reached out her loving arms and said, "Give me a hug right this second and then go to the bathroom, make up your bed, and meet me in the kitchen."

Tenet #5

By choosing to Wake up and MAKE UP your bed, you're learning to wake up to what you can make GO UP in your life.

Chapter 6

Scrambled Eggs and Hands

"**B**reakfast is ready!" Mamaw announced. "Ya'll come on!"

At seemingly just the right moment, Ray, Allen, and Cindy converged on the kitchen. "Ray, grab the napkins and silverware. Allen you get the plates, and Cindy help me by getting the toast out of the oven."

The kitchen was painted with a light green paint color on the walls and cabinets, with a window located right over the sink. There were light red curtains that matched the 1960's diner décor in the breakfast room right off the kitchen. In one corner of the kitchen was the icebox. To the left, in the opposite corner was a pantry that always had plenty of food, but not many sweets. Captain Crunch was always on the top shelf, but on school days, it was always scrambled eggs and toast for breakfast— every day.

As Allen laid the plates out on the table, Ray placed the napkins and forks on the left side of the plates. Mamaw sat the scrambled eggs in the middle of the table and Cindy put a piece of toast on everyone's plate.

"Did everyone wash their hands?" Mamaw asked as she

joined them at the table.

"No ma'am," said Allen.

Ray explained, "My hands aren't dirty."

Cindy and Allen got up to go to the bathroom to wash their hands.

Ray continued with a look of frustration on his face, "For real Mamaw, my hands aren't dirty. I just got out of bed. How can my hands be dirty?"

Mamaw patiently picked up her napkin and said with a smile, "Ray, washing your hands before you eat is more than just about dirty hands. It's about doing first things first. Now go wash your hands and when you come back to the table, we will all talk about why washing your hands matters."

Ray reluctantly got up from the table and headed towards the bathroom that was down the hall from the kitchen. Allen and Cindy returned to the table and Mamaw said, "Let's wait on your brother and then we will pray."

As Ray looked in the mirror while washing his hands, he said to himself, "This is dumb! Why does she make such a big deal about this?" As Ray returned and sat down at the table, Mamaw said, "Let's pray! Cindy, pray for us."

"Dear Heavenly Father, thank you for this food. Bless it to the nourishment of our body. In Jesus name, Amen."

"Pass the ketchup," Allen said.

As Mamaw handed him the ketchup she said, "I want to talk to you sweethearts about why we wash our hands. As I was telling Ray, washing your hands before you come to the table to eat is not about washing your hands because your hands are dirty, although none of us remember or think about where our hands have been before we eat," she said with a smile and a chuckle. She continued, "Washing your hands is about a first things first way of living. One of the most important things in life you will ever need to know is what comes first? Before I continue, let's all draw a scripture."

In the middle of the breakfast table was a little square box that looked like a loaf of bread. This little plastic box had scripture cards sticking upright and every morning Mamaw would encourage everyone to "draw" a scripture out of the box and read it out loud.

Cindy drew her card first and read, "Then God said, 'Let there be light; and there was light.'"

"Cindy honey, go over there," Mamaw said, pointing to the light switch on the wall, "and turn off the light." When Cindy turned the light switch off, the breakfast room was completely dark. "Ok, let's eat. Can somebody pass me the scrambled eggs please?" Mamaw said.

"It's dark Mamaw. We can't see where the eggs are much less eat our food," Ray said.

"Well, we better turn the lights back on," Mamaw said with a smile in her voice.

"Let me ask you a question Ray. Should we turn on the lights first, before we enter this room so we can see what we are going to do next, like eat our food?" Mamaw asked whimsically.

"Of course," he replied.

"That's the same thing God did first, before He did anything else. He turned on the lights, so that what He had next for us could happen."

Scrambled Eggs and Hands

"I have one Mamaw." Allen said. "'But seek first, the kingdom of God and His righteousness, and all these things shall be added to you.'"

"What do you think that means Allen?" Mamaw asked.

"If we put God first, and make His way of doing things our way of doing things, He will add all the other things we need to our lives, wherever and whenever we need it."

"That's right Allen. What God wants us to understand is that He is a God of order and you only get the second things by putting the first things first. Another way of saying it is, when you put first things first, you get the second things thrown in. So, we put God first, and then He throws in all the other things that are important to us.

Ray, what does your verse say?" Mamaw asked.

"God is love."

"Let me ask you a question, and this is for everybody. When God is first in your life, do you think that all of your other relationships will be better?"

Everyone answered in unison, "Yes ma'am."

"Washing our hands before we eat, is about learning what comes first. Doing that not only teaches you about the priority of what comes first, but it prepares you for the second thing, the next thing, and maybe the next thing will be a best thing! So, when we get our priorities right and in order… when we know the first thing we need to do, we can rest assured that what needs to happen second will happen," Mamaw explained.

"And when you wash your hands before you come to the table," Allen said, "you know you are going to GET TO eat!!!!

Mamaw's Tenets for Life

I love to eat! This was so good Mamaw! Thank you for always taking the time to talk to us Mamaw. I love the words you say. They are like food to my soul!"

Cindy smiled and said, "Like the food we are eating is for our body, your words Mamaw are like soul food!"

Scrambled Eggs and Hands

Tenet #6

You get second things only by putting first things first.

Chapter 7

Brush Your Teeth

C indy was always the first to finish her breakfast. "Honey, take your dishes and go ahead and put them in the dishwasher," Mamaw said, "and we need to get going so you're not late to school. Also, everyone be sure to brush your teeth."

As Ray put his dishes in the dishwasher, he thought to himself, "Wash your hands before you eat. Brush your teeth...." He could hear Mamaw's voice even in his head. Every day she would ask those two questions before and after every meal. It seemed like the direction never ended.

"Don't forget to brush your teeth honey," Mamaw said as she reached up and gently rubbed Ray's nose with the knuckles of her fore and middle fingers. This was one of the special ways that Mamaw would connect with her grandchildren. Her soft voice and gentle touch were the spoon full of sugar that made the medicine of her direction be received.

"You know we go to see our dentist later on this week," Mamaw said.

"And we don't want our teeth to rot out between now and then," Ray said with a cynical smile.

Mamaw laughed and said, "No, it's not about your teeth rotting out between now and then. It's about taking care of what you can so that what you take care of, takes care of you!" Mamaw continued, "I have a friend who has false teeth and jokingly she said to me one day, 'If I had known I was going to live this long, I would have taken better care of my teeth!' If you take care of your teeth, your teeth will take care of you. See my teeth," Mamaw said with a big smile, "they didn't get that way all by themselves! Now come on, let's get to school."

Mamaw's Tenets for Life

Tenet #7

What you take care of, will eventually take care of you.

Brush Your Teeth

Chapter 8

Monday Night Meatloaf

Mondays were always a little harder than other days because of Sunday night after church with Aunts, Uncles, and cousins. Mamaw always knew that all 3 children would be especially tired after school. School was out by 3:30, and so Mamaw did something special every Monday night. She fixed her homemade meatloaf.

As Allen walked through the back door he shouted enthusiastically, "Monday Night Meatloaf!!!! Yes!!!"

Mamaw prepared it for everyone, but she always knew Allen would especially enjoy it! It wasn't just the meatloaf, but it was the scalloped potatoes, the fried okra, corn bread with lots of butter, and pinto beans. Even the dinner salad was deliciously prepared with buttermilk dressing.

After putting his books down, Allen grabbed his basketball and said, "Mamaw, I am going to go outside and play awhile."

"Ok honey, but I will probably need you in about an hour to come in and make us some tea and help me set the table."

"Yes, ma'am!" Allen said as he shut the sliding glass door behind him.

The basketball goal was just to the right of the patio. Allen's dad had cut a piece of plywood into the shape of a basketball backboard. He had painted the backboard the same shade of green that the kitchen was painted. Allen didn't care, he just loved to play basketball.

Back in the kitchen, Mamaw continued to prepare the Monday Night Meatloaf when Ray came into the room saying, "Mamaw, I have some homework I have to do tonight and I need your help."

"What can I do for you baby?" Mamaw asked.

"Well, I am supposed to interview someone about the most difficult thing that has ever happened to them and how they got through it. I was thinking about your bout with cancer and how all these years later you struggle with your left arm. I had never noticed you were in pain until that day in the car. And then, when you told us that story... well anyway, I was just wondering if I could interview you for this assignment?"

Mamaw stood at the stove stirring the pinto beans. Her mind went back to that fateful day when she heard the doctor say, "You have breast cancer...." She thought about how it wasn't the cancer that was the most difficult thing that ever happened to her, but what happened in the aftermath of the cancer diagnosis.

In the silence of the moment, the red phone rang in the kitchen. Ray answered the phone. It was his mom saying she was running a few minutes late from work, but would be there as soon as she could. Ray hung up the phone and said, "That was mom, Mamaw. She's running a few minutes late.

So, can I interview you tonight Mamaw?"

"Yes baby. Let's do it after supper. We will eat in about 45 minutes."

Allen heard a car pull up in the driveway on the side of the house that lead to the backyard where he was playing basketball. Gee Whiz, the dog next door, started barking and Allen went to the fence to see who had gotten home. It was Allen's dad, Monroe. He was dressed in his police uniform.

"Hey dad!! How was your day?" Allen asked. Before he could hear his dad say anything, Gee Whiz jumped over the fence. At the same time, Mamaw came outside to ask Allen to come in and help her, but before she could ask him, she heard Gee Whiz yelping.

Gee Whiz was a black and white dog of unknown pedigree, which is why the next-door neighbors had named him Gee Whiz. He was a little bit of this and a little bit of that. He was a very athletic dog and because he could jump the fence, his owners kept him on a leash. They thought it was long enough to keep him from jumping over the fence, but it was a little too long.

Allen and Mamaw ran toward Gee Whiz who was now hanging over the fence by his leash. They both grabbed Gee Whiz and as gently as they could, lowered him onto the neighbor's side of the fence.

"Oh, my goodness Mamaw!!! Allen said. "Gee Whiz almost hung himself. That was so scary!"

"Think of what would have happened if we weren't here," Mamaw said.

"Awe poor Gee Whiz," Allen said as he reached through

Monday Night Meatloaf

the chain-link metal fence. "Come here boy. You can't be doing that! You scared me and almost killed yourself!" Gee Whiz wagged his tail and licked Allen's fingers as if nothing had happened.

About that time, Allen's dad came out of the house and asked, "What happened?"

Allen said, "Gee Whiz almost hanged himself, dad. It was horrible. I'm just so glad Mamaw and I were out here!"

Mamaw had her arm around Allen and said, "You know Allen, everyone has a leash like Gee Whiz."

"What?" Allen asked, "What do you mean Mamaw?"

Mamaw replied, "It's your God given conscience."

"So, if we all have a leash, what is it and why can't I see it?" Allen asked.

"I'm hungry," Allen's dad said.

"Me too!" said Allen. "And dad, it's Monday night and you know what that means, right?"

"I sure do," said Monroe. "It means Monday Night Meat-loaf!"

Allen hugged his dad, and as he did he said, "Mamaw let's talk about that leash thing over our meatloaf, ok?"

"We sure can Allen," Mamaw said, "but right now I need you to come in and make us some tea. Let's get ready to eat. Your mom will be home any minute."

Chapter 9

The Law of the Leash

"**M**ommy's home!" Cindy said as she came into the kitchen.

Cindy's mom, Gayle, was a personal assistant to a high-level CEO of a large corporation. She would arrive home around 5:30 every Monday through Friday. Recently, she had been featured in the local major newspaper as one of the city's most beautiful women. With 3 children and a full-time job, she was grateful to have her mother living with her.

Monday nights were very special not only because of Mamaw's famous meatloaf, but because it was a special time for the family to eat together. More important than the fabulous food were the family talks that would take place.

"Mom, you will never believe what happened today." Allen said.

"What happened?" Gayle asked.

"You know how Gee Whiz was always jumping over the fence and the Greens decided to put a leash on him. Well, today, I'm outside shooting hoops, and I hear dad pull up in the driveway, so I was saying 'Hi' to him when all-of-a-sudden, I heard Gee Whiz yelping. I turned around and he had jumped over our fence, like he always did, but this time, he had a leash on!"

"Oh my," said Gayle.

"Next thing I know, Mamaw came running and we grabbed Gee Whiz and lifted him back over the fence."

Gayle asked, "Was he ok?"

"Yes ma'am," Allen answered, "but if we hadn't been out there, he would have hanged himself over our fence."

"Oh, I am so glad you and Mamaw were there and I'm so glad Gee Whiz is ok," she said with a smile as she took a bite of her meatloaf.

"Mamaw, tell Mom what you were saying about the leash," Allen said.

"What about the leash?" Ray asked.

Before Mamaw could say anything, Allen said, "Mamaw said we all have a leash."

"I don't have a leash," Cindy said with a perplexed look on her face."

"Well I used to have a leash," Ray said.

Monroe, the children's dad, laughed and said, "You sure did! By the time your brother Ray was two years old, he could climb our chain-link fence."

"That's crazy," Allen said.

"Yes, it was crazy," said Gayle. "One Saturday morning, your dad and I were sleeping late when I heard the phone ring. On the other end of the line was the manager of a store about 4 blocks from our house who said, 'Did you know your two-year-old son is in my store asking for candy? He's standing right here in front of me at the counter in his diaper and he keeps looking at me saying, "Candy... Candy." I just thought I would let you know!'"

Everyone at the table was laughing out loud. "So, we had to get him a leash. I would leash him to the clothes line in our backyard and he would run back and forth, back and forth, back and forth, but it cured him from climbing the fence! I'm not sure what all the neighbors thought, but we had a law for Ray, and that was, if he was going outside, he was going to be wearing a leash, for his protection and our peace of mind." Gayle said with a sigh and a smile.

"Well, I don't have a leash," Cindy said again.

And Allen chimed, "I don't either, but I guess some people need a leash. But you said everybody has a leash Mamaw."

"Well everybody does Allen. As I said, it's your God-given conscience. You see, our conscience is our awareness. You can't see your conscience, but God gave you your conscience to help you be aware of what is right and wrong, what is good and bad. Studies have been done by researchers at the Harvard Medical School, and they have discovered that our brainstem that extends from our spinal cord is our internal leash. It controls our breathing, our heart function, and even when we go to sleep and wake up."

Mamaw continued, "So, when there is damage to the spinal cord that effects the brainstem, people become comatose or unconscious. But our conscience is more than a physical reality. Our conscience not only comes from God, but our conscience proves God. Just like there are physical laws like gravity that govern what we can see, there are spiritual laws that govern the parts of the world, and us, that we cannot see.

The Law of the Leash

I call our conscience, or ability to be conscious, the law of the leash. The law of the leash says, 'Everybody has enough of a leash to succeed or fail, to do right or to do wrong, to help themselves or hang themselves.'

I believe God gave us our lungs to direct our oxygen anywhere we want it to go. I believe God gave us our heart, so that it could direct blood to every part of our body, so that our bodies bring glory and honor to Him. Most importantly, I believe God gave us our conscience, so that as we become more aware of Him, we would choose to live and move and find our very being in Him.

Gee Whiz had a leash, but his leash didn't help him."

"Why not Mamaw?" Allen asked.

"Because that is what separates us from animals. We not only have a conscience given to us by God, but our conscience makes us consciously aware of fences we are not supposed to jump over," Mamaw said with an emphatic grin. "Gee Whiz has a fence for his protection. Inside that fence is water, food, shelter, and companionship with people that want him as their pet. Outside of that fence is a much harder life. He would have to find his own food, water, and shelter. Outside that fence he would have to find someone who would want him for a pet. The fence is for him! But he doesn't know it! And that's the difference between dogs and humans. You can love a dog or a pet like a human, but a pet can only love you like a pet, because he's not human."

Mamaw continued, "Like Gee Whiz and the fence, God gives us boundaries. Those boundaries are not to punish us, but to bless us. The leash of our conscience is not to restrain us, but to protect us. When we become consciously aware of what is good and evil, when we know the difference between what is best and what is worst, what would help us and what would hurt us, spirit, soul and body, and we make the right decision, we help ourselves and not hurt ourselves like Gee Whiz did."

"How do you always know what is right or wrong?" Ray asked, "or what will help you or hurt you?"

"Or what will make you not hang yourself like Gee Whiz did," asked Cindy.

"Monroe," Mamaw asked, "isn't it true that in every country of the world stealing is against the law?"

"Yes ma'am," he answered.

"Isn't it true that in every country of the world murdering someone is against the law?"

"Yes ma'am."

Mamaw looked at each one of the children and asked, "Is it always wrong to lie?"

"Yes ma'am, they answered in unison."

"There are certain things that all people, in all cultures, throughout history have known were wrong. This fact is more than just moral law, but it is spiritual or eternal law, that applies in natural law, and yet, I believe that it proves God's existence in humanity, because everyone is consciously aware that if they cross those "fences" and commit those acts, they hurt themselves and others. The law of the leash is based on the Bible, not just as moral law, but spiritual laws that help us set boundaries, so our lives are healthy, happy, and blessed."

Tenet #8

Everybody has enough of a leash to succeed or fail, to do right or to do wrong, to help themselves or hang themselves.

Chapter 10

Great-Full

"This is amazing, Mother," Gayle said. The table grew momentarily quiet, as everyone savored the moment and enjoyed their food.

Allen took his corn bread and grabbed the butter. "I love everything about this meal Mamaw. I know you do this just for me! I am so grateful!" Allen said with a gleaming smile.

"She does it for all of us," Gayle said, "but she makes each one of us feel so special, like it's just for us."

"Yes, thank you so much Mamaw," Monroe said, as he took a bite of fried okra. "This is my personal favorite. I don't know how you get the batter perfect every time, but you do, and it's so good!"

"My favorite is the scalloped potatoes," Cindy said, "I love all the cheese!"

"Thank you all for expressing your gratitude. I believe when you are grateful, your life will be GREAT-FULL."[1] Mamaw said with a smile, "And You are right Allen, it's just for you. I love making you all this special meal on Monday nights, but more than that, I appreciate your heart of gratitude. I have discovered that gratitude is an energy-producing magnet that draws more of what you want and value towards you."[2]

"So, the more grateful I am for meatloaf the more meatloaf I get?" Allen asked.

"Well, yes, it's that and a whole lot more! There is actually scientific research that shows all kinds of benefits come from being grateful."

"I love science," Cindy said, "tell us some of the benefits Mamaw."

"I can tell you that growing up with Mamaw as my mother was one of the greatest gifts God ever gave me." Gayle said. "Yes, Mamaw, do share some of those scientific benefits with us."

Allen interrupted and said, "I need to go get me some more tea. Can I be excused from the table mom?"

"Yes, and Mamaw is going to go ahead and share with us, so let's listen."

"First of all," Mamaw began, "being grateful helps you make new friendships, even when you are not trying to. When you express gratitude, Allen, it makes people feel appreciated. When people feel appreciated they want to do things for you and be around you.[3]

Second, being grateful improves your physical health. Grateful people experience less aches and pains.[4] In another study, 186 men and women around the age of 66, who had all suffered some sort of heart damage, filled out a questionnaire asking about the people, places, and things they most appreciated. The researchers found that those people who were most grateful were less depressed, slept better, were more energetic, and, after a blood test, showed the lowest levels of heart inflammation and plaque buildup in their arteries. A follow-up revealed that patients who kept a gratitude journal for two months showed reduced inflammation and improved heart rhythm."

"That's amazing!" Monroe said. "Please continue Mamaw."

"Third, being grateful improves your self-esteem. Grateful people are able to celebrate other people's accomplishments. That's why we want to be grateful for anything good in others that leads to them doing well in their life. Unfortunately, ungrateful people are negative and resentful towards people who accomplish more or have more than they."

"So, I should be grateful that Allen beat me for the first time in a game of basketball yesterday?" Ray asked with a hint of doubt in his voice.

"Well you know Ray, I am going to get a college scholarship someday to play basketball!!" Allen said confidently. "I know that's not your dream, but it is mine."

Mamaw said, "Yes, Ray, that's exactly what you should celebrate, because if you do, you may be the one who helped him reach his dream. There are so many benefits to gratitude. I could go on and on, but I want to stop and say to each of you how grateful I am to be a part of this precious family. Monroe, I especially appreciate you as my daughter's husband. You have always done so much for me, and with what happened with Papaw...."

With that Mamaw paused and said, "I am just so grateful, and because of all of you, my life is GREAT-FULL!

I need to give you one more benefit of gratitude. This

one is a secret that only those who have been through severe trauma of some kind can really appreciate. Being grateful, even in the worst and most difficult times of your life, supernaturally endows you with a spirit of resilience. One of my favorite scriptures in the Bible is *'In everything give thanks; for this is the will of God in Christ Jesus for you.'"*

Mamaw continued, "When I begin to feel sorry for myself or I find myself focusing on the things I think I deserve, with God's help I just stop and focus on what I do have, and I give thanks, with a grateful heart. Being at this table with all of you is my heaven on earth, and I am so grateful."

Endnotes

1 @Leadershipology, keithcraft.org

2 @Leadershipology, keithcraft.org

3 Study published in *Emotion, 2014*

4 Published in *Personality and Individual Differences, 2012*

Tenet #9

When you are grateful, your life will be GREAT-FULL.

Chapter 11

The Aftermath

"Mamaw, can I do the interview with you for school?" Ray asked.

"Yes, honey. I'm almost finished with the kitchen. Let's go into the den."

The den was right off the kitchen to the left. It was the back of the house where the sliding glass doors were that led outside. You could stand in the den and see all the way to the front of the house. The den was separated from the dining room by French doors that remained open unless there were guest over for a special dinner. You could also see into the front room, which was the formal living room.

As Mamaw nestled herself into her favorite chair, Ray came and sat beside her. He said, "I'm going to record this so I can make sure I get everything."

Mamaw begin to think about what she was going to say, and more importantly, what she wasn't going to say. No one in the family ever talked much about Papaw. He and Mamaw had divorced years before and he chose not to be in any of the grandchildren's lives.

"Okay Mamaw, are you ready?" Ray asked.

"Yes, sweetheart if you are," she said with a familiar smile on her face. "I'm just going to lay my chair back and close my eyes while I talk, ok?"

"Sure!" Ray said. "Here we go!"

Mamaw spoke softly, with her head laid back and her eyes closed. "1956 was quite the year. When the doctor said, 'You have breast cancer...' those words were the most difficult words I had ever heard someone say to me up until that point. You see, Ray honey, hearing the doctor say that and how the next few months of exploratory laser treatment would affect me were not the most difficult thing I was to face. It was the aftermath."

"What?" Ray interrupted, "what could be worse than that?"

"I've never told anybody except your mother this. Your Papaw didn't go to church much. But when he found out I had cancer, he told God he would go if God would heal me."

"What happened Mamaw?" Ray asked solemnly.

"Your Papaw lost his faith, and when he lost his faith, he lost his way and made the decision to leave me."

Ray noticed tears streaming down Mamaw's face, even though her eyes were closed. He could hear the pain in her voice. "Awe Mamaw... are you ok? I'm so sorry," Ray said.

With that, Mamaw raised her chair back up and opened her tear-filled eyes. She took a Kleenex with her right hand, while she raised her glasses from her face with her injured arm. "I loved your Papaw so much, and I still do."

"Did you ever see him again Mamaw?" Ray asked as he reached over and took Mamaw by the hand.

"No honey, I never did see him again. But the Lord is so

good. The most difficult thing I have ever had to face is your Papaw leaving me and losing his hope in God."

Mamaw reached over with her injured arm and gently caressed the tip of Ray's nose with her hand. He could smell the fresh scent of moisturizer she always kept on her hands. Her touch was as close to a soft feather pillow that he had ever felt.

"How did you get through it Mamaw?" Ray asked.

"First, baby, God gave me strength when I was at my weakest point. His Word says, 'My grace is all you need. My power works best in weakness... for when I am weak, then I am strong'.[1]

Second, my family of origin and my church, my family of choice, gave me strength. They loved me, they encouraged me, and they upheld me when I couldn't hold myself up. They prayed for me, for Papaw, and for my broken heart. I forgave him immediately, but it took some time for my heart to be healed. I realized you cannot control what other people do to you, but you can control what you do to others. I prayed for him every day until he passed away.

Third, God answered my prayer for Papaw. I prayed that his faith would be restored. Your Uncle Ernest went to see him before he passed away and he asked Papaw if he had made things right between him and God. Papaw couldn't speak, but as your uncle held his hand, tears began to come out of his eyes, as he nodded his head, yes. God is so good Ray. In the last hours of his life, God touched Papaw and his faith was restored."

Mamaw leaned forward again towards Ray and said, "Al-

The Aftermath

ways remember Ray, God is faithful!"

That night, as Ray laid in his bunk bed, his heart was filled with gratitude for his sweet Mamaw... and for the faithfulness of God.

Endnotes

1 *2 Corinthians 12:9,12b*

Tenet #10

You cannot control what other people do to you, but you can control what you do to others.

Tenet #11

God is faithful.

Chapter 12
'69 Cuda

"**A**llen, come get in the car," Allen's dad said enthusiastically.

"Where are we going dad?" Allen asked.

"Just get in," his dad said, "it's going to be fun!"

Allen knew it was going to be fun because the car his dad asked him to get into was a 1969 Barracuda. This wasn't your average car, not by a long shot. It was painted in a custom purple with black interior. This was the first year the Plymouth Barracuda would be called the "Cuda." The "Cuda Performance Package" included a high-performance drivetrain, heavy duty suspension and wheels, dual exhaust, plus blackout trim and sport tape stripes, and a pair of hood scoops. There were only 272 Barracudas known as the Formula S ever built.

But it was the interior of the car and what was on the dashboard that always got Allen's attention. The speedometer went up to 150 miles per hour! This car was the epitome of fun for Allen.

As Allen crawled into the cockpit of the '69 Cuda, his heart raced. "This is so cool dad... cool!" Allen exclaimed.

"I know how much you like it Allen and that's why I wanted us to take a ride today. You are actually going to drive today." his dad said.

"What? Dad you are going to let me drive?" Allen said with a gigantic smile on his face.

"Yes, I am! You can't tell anybody, especially your mother!" Monroe the Cop said.

Even though Allen was only 13, he and his dad were about the same height. Monroe, who was a policeman, had taken Allen driving many times on remote farm roads since he was about 11. But today was a special treat. Today, Allen would drive the '69 Cuda for the first time.

It was early Saturday morning, and after about an hour and with no cars in sight, Allen's dad said, "Are you ready?"

"Yes sir!"

Allen's dad pulled the car over to the side of the road and they switched places. As Allen slid into the driver's side seat of the Cuda, he felt goose bumps all over him. "Dad, I just can't believe this. I am so excited!"

"I am excited for you Allen," his dad said, "just be careful. Let's watch the speed limit."

"Don't worry about that dad." Allen replied.

"Keep both hands on the wheel after you switch gears and keep driving north for a while. As long as there are no cars on the road, I will let you drive."

Allen pressed the clutch, and as he put the Cuda in gear and pressed the gas, he thought to himself, "This is heaven on earth." After only a few minutes of driving, Allen looked over only to see his father had fallen asleep. As a policeman, he worked a variety of shifts that required him to get rest when he could. He worked several jobs to provide the life he wanted his family to have. He bought cars like the Cuda on the side and would fix them up and sell them. He worked some real estate as well. In fact, the house that the family lived in was moved from a more expensive part of town. Monroe also had a distant uncle that owned a Sinclair Gas Station, and that's where he would work on cars.

As he continued to drive north from Dallas, Texas, he had no idea what their destination would be, but Allen was enjoying every moment. Mamaw had taught him to "Seize the Moment" and always take a picture. Today was one of those moments and he was so glad he remembered to bring his camera. His mind raced as he drove along, and yet, as his dad softly snored next to him, Allen thought, "I love my dad. I know he is doing this just for me. This is so much fun!"

The sound of the engine... the feel of the car... in that moment, Allen felt special. He began to think about some of the recent fun times he and his dad had shared. He thought about how different he was from his dad, but how his dad celebrated his being who he was. His dad never tried to make him feel different, in fact, he would just say, "I don't care what we do together, I just want to be with you."

Allen remembered how recently, they were at the Sinclair Gas Station where he was watching his dad work on a car. Monroe had the hood open with a light hanging from the underside of the hood. Allen remembered thinking how smart his dad was to be able to know what was wrong with a car and fix it. He recalled his dad saying with his head down working on the engine, "Hey Allen, hand me a Phillips-head."

As Allen thought about this, he laughed out loud as he drove along. "What's a Phillips-head dad?"

His dad lifted up his head from the engine and said in a shocked voice, "Do you not know what a Phillips-head screwdriver is son?"

"No sir!" Allen remembered saying.

His dad smiled and walked patiently over to the big red tool box and held up two screwdrivers. "Son, this is a Phillips-head and this is a flat-head. Do you see the difference?"

"Yes sir." Allen smiled as he remembered.

"Now you know." Allen laughed out loud again as he drove along, and this time, it woke up his dad.

"What are you laughing about son?" his dad said with a tired smile.

"The screwdriver thing that happened recently dad," Allen said with a laugh.

"Yes, that was funny son. You are funny to me without trying to be," Allen's dad said, "that's one of the many reasons I like being with you." With that, Monroe laid his head back and fell fast asleep.

Mamaw's Tenets for Life

Tenet #12

Seize the Moment and always take a
picture.

Chapter 13

Meet the Past

"D ad, I think we need to stop for gas," Allen said.
Allen's dad slowly opened his eyes and said,
"How long did I sleep?"

"I've been driving for about two hours I think, but just
noticed we need to get gas," Allen responded.

"Pull over at the next exit" Monroe said with a big yawn.
"I must have been tired son. How are you doing? Has everything gone well?"

"Yes, sir. I just kept driving and have loved every second,
dad." Allen said.

They pulled into the gas station. "Go ahead and get Reg-
ular and I will also add some octane booster. This engine is
high performance and needs it," Monroe said.

"Can I get a Coke dad?"

"Sure son. Let's both get one." Monroe answered.

As they walked back towards the car, drinking their
Cokes, Allen said, "Dad, I love Coke! I love the taste from the
bottle. I love the burn. Thanks Dad."

"Your welcome son. Hey, I will drive the rest of the way,
we are almost there."

"Where are we going dad, you haven't even told me." Allen said.

"You will see son," Monroe said. "Let me grab my camera dad and take a picture. You know what Mamaw always says, 'Seize the Moment and always take a picture!'" Allen hurriedly grabbed his camera. It had been sitting right under the gear shift on the console the whole time.

"Dad, stand right there."

Allen's dad paused and said, "Don't just get me in the picture, let's get somebody to take it, so we can both be in it."

"Ok." And with that, Allen turned around and saw a guy on a Harley Davidson pull up to the pump next to them. Before Allen could ask him to take the picture, the guy said, "What a cool Cuda! Can I get a picture with it?"

"Sure," Allen answered "and then maybe you could take a picture of my dad and me."

It was only about 30 minutes later that Allen and his dad pulled into Muscogee, Oklahoma. Allen knew his dad was from here, but they didn't talk about it much. They drove into a very run-down neighborhood. In fact, he had never seen a more impoverished place in his short life. As they turned down a street, he noticed most of the houses had been abandoned. There were boards on the windows and doors. The car came to a stop in front of a small, dilapidated white house. Instead of a front door, there was a mangled screen door and there was no glass on the windows.

Allen got out of the car and held his dad's hand as they walked towards the house. Without saying anything, Allen's dad led them into the house.

Allen noticed immediately that there was a dirt floor, and he saw a few animals. And then over in the corner, on the only piece of furniture in the room, sat an old man. Allen's dad walked them over to the man and he said, "Hello dad. This is my son Allen."

The man didn't look at Allen or speak. His mouth slightly opened and Allen could see that he had no teeth. Allen thought, "This is my dad's dad?" He felt a little uncomfortable, so he walked away as he heard his dad say, "I brought you some money and candy."

Allen looked around only for a few moments as he headed towards the entry of the house to step outside. In just a few minutes, Allen's dad came through the door with a look of concern on his face. Allen took his dad's hand and said, "I don't ever want to come back here dad."

"That's why I brought you here son, because this is where we are from, but this is not who we are."

They walked to the car and drove away. As they headed back towards Dallas, Allen's dad told him more about how he grew up and how his dad left when he was very young. He told him he didn't even really know about how a family was supposed be, but Monroe told Allen he knew he didn't want that. He talked about how, when he met Mamaw, she showed him a type of love he had never known. He talked about how she told him, "Where you are from is not who you are." Allen's dad told him for the first time, that when he met Gayle, Allen's mother, he didn't just meet his wife, but he met his family of choice. He talked about how Gayle's 2 brothers and sister had become the 2 brothers and sister he never had.

Meet the Past

On the drive home, Allen didn't think about the car. He thought about the connect that he and his dad had. He thought about how his dad had used the '69 Cuda to show him where he was from, but more importantly, to show Allen who he was and who his family was, and he thought, "I will remember this moment and I will always remember this picture of this '69 Cuda day."

Tenet #13

Where you are from is not who you are.

Chapter 14

Mamaw Appreciation Day

I n the summer of 1992, Mamaw was now 80 years old
and was about to get a glimpse of heaven, without having to die to go to heaven. Ray was 34 and married with two
children. Allen was 32, married and had 3 children. In fact,
Ray and Allen had married sisters. Cindy was married. Gayle
and Monroe were retired, living in a small east Texas town.

Allen had called the entire family together, not for a fam-
ily reunion, but for a Mamaw Appreciation Day. Gayle was
Mamaw's daughter and she had 3 siblings, an older brother
Ernest, a sister Anne, and a younger brother named David.
They all were married and had children, and some of their
children had children.

They came from various parts of Texas to honor Mamaw,
their mother and grandmother, who had made such an incredible impact on their lives. Forty-five family members
gathered in a small but luxurious Banquet Ballroom of a ho-
tel in Arlington, Texas.

The tables were beautifully decorated beginning with a
matelassé' linen table cloth that was white. Ray and Allen's
wives made sure that this night would be like a banquet at

Buckingham Palace, fit for a Queen. The linen napkins were folded in the shape of a Dutch Bonnet with a hand embroidered monogram showing an "M." The chairs were placed exactly 27 inches from the table and each draped with a silk bow on the backs of each seat.

The center pieces were large urns with white and green flowers, white garden roses, blooming branches and arrangements of birch, beech, and hornbeam.

The dinnerware was antique silver and cut crystal, indeed fit for the Queen... Mamaw.

As everyone came into the banquet room, the first thing they did was stop and look. The ceiling was draped with a sheer Voile Chiffon ceiling drape. The most impressive thing in the room was the single chair on an elevated stage just for Mamaw. The chair was made of beechwood and was carved and gilded. It was a high back English chair that was fashioned after Queen Elizabeth's 1953 Coronation Chair. The upholstery was blue silk with a tasseled white fringing. The chair was embroidered with an "M" and had an embroidered crown on top of the "M."

Allen waited backstage with Mamaw because he wanted her to have a grand entrance.

Ray pulled the curtain back and said, "Hey Allen, everyone is here. Are you and Mamaw ready?" he asked with a big smile.

"Mamaw, are you ready?" Allen asked.

Mamaw had no idea what was about to happen. She hadn't seen the room and didn't know who was going to be there. In fact, she didn't even know why she was there.

All of the sudden Ray said, "Ladies and Gentlemen, I want to welcome you to a very special occasion. We are all here because of this person, and we are here to honor her tonight. Would everyone join me and show your love and appreciation for our Mamaw!"

With that, Allen pulled the curtain back and led Mamaw out onto the elevated stage. Everyone was clapping and cheering. Mamaw was so shocked and surprised! She turned to Allen and asked, "Why is everyone I love here, honey?"

And while everyone was still clapping and cheering, Allen said, "We are all here to honor you, Mamaw. Welcome to Mamaw Appreciation Day!"

Chapter 15

Let the Honor Begin

A new song by Amy Grant was playing in the background as everyone gathered around Mamaw to love on her.

"Breath of Heaven ... Hold me together... Be forever near me... Breath of Heaven... Breath of Heaven... Lighten my darkness... Pour over me your holiness... For you are holy... Breath of Heaven. . . . "

"Do you hear that song?" Mamaw asked as everyone grew silent. "That's what I am feeling right now. Have I died and gone to heaven?"

Everyone smiled. Joy and laughter filled the room as the families began to greet one another. Allen stepped up on the elevated platform where Mamaw's Royal Chair awaited her and said, "If I could have everyone's attention, I would like to talk about what is going to happen tonight. As you know, we are all here to honor Mamaw." And with that statement, Allen was moved to tears.

"Mamaw, this is your night. It's all about you. Every person here has been the beneficiary of your love, your servant's heart, your caring ways, and most importantly, your godly life that you have lived in front of us all. Tonight, we wanted you to have a little bit of heaven on earth while you are still alive and well. We all love you so much."

Allen continued, "To all the family, I want to say a heartfelt 'Thank you' for being here to honor our sweet Mamaw. What will happen tonight is we will all eat together and have a time of fellowship and catching up. After we get through eating, we will invite Mamaw up to the stage and she will sit in her Royal Chair while we will go around the room and share what she means to us. There is no pressure for anyone to say anything, but we just want to make sure you know we would like you to, if you want to. I also want to draw your attention to the tree beside the Royal Chair. That is a Money Tree. I want to invite you as you come on stage to share your heart with Mamaw, that you put your money where your mouth is and let's all bless her tonight." Everyone laughed and Allen said, "Now let's eat. Let's talk. Let's have a great time, and then, Let the Honor Begin."

Everyone moved to their respective tables and for the next hour, joyful chatter filled the air. Allen greeted each table and asked each of Mamaw's children if they would share something they most appreciated about Mamaw.

After dinner Allen helped Mamaw to her Royal Chair and as he did, Ray and Cindy presented her with a dozen beautiful red roses.

"Oh babies, thank you so much. I just don't know what to say. I don't feel like I deserve this." Both of them hugged her and kissed her.

"Mother I want to go first," Ernest said. "You were the

greatest mother anyone could ever have. On this auspicious occasion, I want to thank you for every sacrifice you made, the ones I know about and the ones I don't know about. You helped me become the man I am. The fact that God chose you to be my mother is proof of how much He loves me. Thank you, Mother," he begins to cry, "Thank you for everything you've done for me and for who you are to me. I love you so much and will be eternally grateful for you."

"I'll go next," Gayle said. "I have always felt extravagantly loved by you and that's why I guess I love you so much. You have been my confidant when I had no one else to talk to. You have been my encourager in my darkest hours. You have been my example of what a woman of God looks like and acts like. You made sure that we went to church. You prayed for us and with us. You gave me a love for the Word of God. Thank you, Mother, for always being there for me, no matter what. You are the best mother in the world."

"Well I guess we are going in the order of our birth, so I will go next," Jane said with a big smile on her face. "Mother you were continually optimistic, no matter how pessimistic everyone around you was. You encouraged us to look on the bright side of life." Jane's voice begins to shake with loving emotion, "You did not believe anything but the best of people and you taught me to do the same. You taught us, 'If you can't say something good, don't say it.' Mother, you taught us to love well, because you loved us well. Thank you for being my loving mother."

By now, Mamaw's eyes were filled with tears of joy. Her presence almost seemed angelic as she sat stately in her Roy-

Let the Honor Begin

al Chair. As she wiped the tears from her eyes, David stood up.

"Mother…" he said, as his voiced cracked, "you have more faith than anyone I have ever known. I feel like you could have written the book of Hebrews in the Bible. I am sure you are in God's Faith Hall of Fame. You have been through so many trials, almost like Job in the bible, and you have come out a winner every time. I know everyone here, all your children, grandchildren, and even your great grandchildren, feel that a better woman could not be found. A better attitude could not be found. And for sure, a better mother and Mamaw they could never find. Thank you, Mother. You are truly THE BEST!"

It was a night that Mamaw would never forget, as almost every family member honored her for the person that she was and the profound impact she had made on and in each of their lives.

Mamaw's Tenets for Life

Tenet #14

If you don't have something good to
say, don't say it.

*Mamaw at her
Appreciation Day.*

*Mamaw with Ray (my brother) and
his spouse; me and Sheila; mom
and dad; and Cindy (my sister).*

*Gayle (my mom) and Mamaw (her
mom).*

*Mamaw with Ray (my brother on
the left); Cindy (my sister); and me
(on the right).*

Chapter 16

Mamaw's Greatest Hits

I t was Mother's Day, Sunday May 9, 1999. Allen drove up in front of his parents' house in Emory, Texas. Emory is about 65 miles from Dallas, a small tight-knit community with towering pine trees. Allen's parents had moved there when they retired. Mamaw, now 87, lived with them.

"Mamaw, can I come in?" Allen asked as he stood at the bedroom door.

"Yes, baby, please do!" Mamaw answered with delight in her voice.

"Happy Mother's Day Mamaw," Allen said as he reached down and gave her a kiss. Mamaw reached up and gave Allen her all familiar nose touch. Allen immediately felt her loving spirit connect deeply with him.

"I wanted to come see you on this special day, Mamaw. I love you so much. How are you feeling?" Allen asked.

"Oh honey, God is so good to me. I'm feeling pretty good. I've been reading my bible today and I just keep saying one of my favorite scriptures over and over."

As Allen sat down next to Mamaw, he knew she was so weak, and yet her presence made him feel so strong. Her health had begun to deteriorate, but it had no impact on her positive spirit and her bright smiling face.

"Yes, baby I just keep saying 'This is the day that the Lord has made; let us rejoice and be glad in it." Mamaw paused and took Allen's hand and said, "I am so glad you are here sweetheart."

"I am so glad too, Mamaw, that I could be here."

"How was church today baby?" she asked.

"It was amazing Mamaw! But beyond the fact that I wanted to love on you, I want to talk to you about why I'm here," Allen said with a smile.

"I have this journal with me and I want to ask you to do something for me." Allen said.

"Ok, what do you want me to do honey?"

"Well Mamaw," Allen began, "all the pages in this journal are blank, and I have asked a question at the top of each page I would like for you to answer." As he opened the journal, Allen showed her the questions at the top of blank page.

He continued, "And I have thought about these questions a lot, and I want you to answer with as much detail as you are comfortable with." Allen said with a soft smile. "In fact, Mamaw, the only thing that has been printed in this journal is Psalm 118:24, the scripture that you have been saying all day. Look! It's printed right here on the front page of the journal."

"Isn't that amazing Allen?" Mamaw asked with a beaming smile. "You know I really believe that when you have a favorite verse, it leads to a favored life."

"Yes, it is amazing Mamaw. You have taught me that. You have taught our whole family to love the Word of God, and like a Light, to let it lead us. For all those years, every morning at breakfast before school, you would have us draw a scripture out of the Bread of Life, little plastic loaf of bread thing." Allen said as he fondly remembered those special times. "Do you remember what my favorite scripture was way back then?" Allen asked.

"I sure do Allen," Mamaw said without a pause. "It was Deuteronomy 33:27, *'The eternal God is your refuge, and underneath are the everlasting arms; He will thrust out the enemy before you, and will say, 'Destroy!'*

"Wow, Mamaw, you are amazing! How do you remember that?" Allen asked.

"Because it's one of my favorites too, just like you Allen. You are one of my favorites!" Mamaw said.

In that moment, Allen felt a physical feeling of her love inside his body. It was like drinking a warm hot chocolate on a cold day. "I am your favorite, Mamaw, and anyone who doesn't believe me can ask me," Allen said with a laugh.

As Allen opened the journal he explained, "At the top of every page I have written a question for you to answer, Mamaw. This little book will be 'Mamaw's Greatest Hits'! There are questions about your childhood memories, about how you met your husband, why you named your kids what you did, things that matter most to you, and even a question about your favorite recipes. Some of the questions are pretty intimate Mamaw," Allen said with a smile. "Who was your first kiss, who was your first boyfriend, what was the happiest time in your life, what was the hardest day of your life, and then what advice you would want others to remember, and what kind of legacy you want to leave, and more."

"Wow, that seems like a lot to think about, but I will look forward to doing it," Mamaw said.

"Yes ma'am, it will be for our family. It will be your life story in your own words. It will be a compilation of Mamaw's Greatest Hits!" Allen exclaimed.

"Well I don't know honey if it will be about greatest hits, but I will be glad to do it for you," Mamaw said.

"Thank you so much Mamaw. There's no rush, just work on it when you can, Ok?" Allen asked.

"Yes, baby, I will do that. Now let's eat something. Are you hungry?" Mamaw asked.

"You know me Mamaw. I'm always hungry and I am so glad I GET TO eat with you!"

Tenet #15

When you have a favorite verse, it will lead to a favored life.

Chapter 17

The Greatest Life Lessons

As Mamaw opened her new journal, she noticed Allen had written the following words on the opening page:

Reflections from Mamaw's Heart
Your Life Story in Your Own Words

She saw the only thing that was pre-printed at the bottom of the opening page was Psalm 118:24:

"This is the day the Lord has made; let us rejoice and be glad in it."

As she turned to the next page, she saw in Allen's handwriting:

Mamaw's Memories

She began to write about her life and memories. Her mind went back to the "Issacs Mountains" in eastern Oklahoma where she was raised. She answered questions about her parents, who she called "Papa and Mama." She listed some of her favorite memories as a child, including listening to her father play the banjo and how she loved to dance to his music.

One of her favorite memories was praying at her mother's knee. She recounted how they had church in their house and local Indians would come. She even learned to speak Cherokee. Her father was a farmer, and her hero. She wrote about her genealogy and what it was like to grow up with four sisters and 3 brothers.

Page after page she filled with beautiful memories about the people and places from her childhood. Then, she came to the page that said:

Recall some of the Greatest Life Lessons you have learned

Mamaw laid down her pen and leaned back in her big recliner chair. "Greatest Life Lessons..." she said to herself. "My life lessons could be a book all by themselves." Her mind remembered something her papa had said to her one day while they were picking cotton together. One of the reasons he was her hero was because they always talked about everything. She loved how he never missed an opportunity to connect with her while they worked hard on the farm. She remembered one conversation about cotton....

"You know Becky, it's up to us to know how to use this cotton God has blessed us with. Cotton is a lot like life. It's not just this, it's a this and that. Did you know that cotton is both a fiber and a food? The pants I'm wearing and the dress your wearing are made of cotton. But also, cotton seed is used to feed cattle and crushed to make oil. It's up to us to know how to use what God has given us in life and for life. Life is about learning, and when we learn not just what something is, but how it can be used, we have a Life Lesson."

Then, she remembered him saying something she would never forget: "Our life lessons are our life lessons. If we learn them, everyone becomes the beneficiary. If we don't learn our life lessons, everyone in our life will have to deal with our lack, rather than what we were supposed to have learned."

She began to reflect on the many Life Lessons she had learned on the farm, but she had never identified what her Greatest Life Lessons were, until now. She picked her pen up and began to write:

1. I have learned to Honor God first.

2. When I open my eyes in the morning I say, 'This is the day the Lord has made; I will rejoice and I will be glad in it.'

3. I have learned to pray for God's perfect will to be done in my life and in my loved one's lives, and that when I ask the Holy Spirit to lead me, He does.

4. I have learned to be content in whatever state I am in because no matter what it looks like, I know God loves me and will never leave me.

5. I have learned to be thoughtful and treat others as I would like to be treated.

6. I have learned to thank God every day for His peace and joy in my life, even when there seems to be no reason.

7. I have learned that when I am thankful, God helps me not to be griping and mean when I am in pain.

8. I have learned that when I cast my burdens and problems on the Lord, that's when He gives me strength and shows me His way of life.

As she concluded her Greatest Life Lessons, there was a knock at her door. "Mother," Gayle asked, as she opened the door quietly, "would you like some buttermilk and cornbread?"

"How did you know I wanted some of my favorite food right now?" Mamaw asked with a smile.

"Because I know you and I know what you like," Gayle said as she laid the tv tray in Mamaw's lap. "I already put butter on the cornbread and it's melted and ready for you. How's your journaling coming?"

"It's wonderful honey. I am having the best time remembering. I have so many beautiful memories," Mamaw said.

"I am so glad you are doing that Mother, so we have your story in your own words. Enjoy your snack and I will see you in the morning. I love you."

"I love you too, honey. Thank you! This is so good!"

Tenet #16

Your life lessons are your life lessons. If you learn them well, everyone around you will benefit.

Chapter 18

The Greatest Summer Day

A s Mamaw lay in bed the next morning, she could see the sun beaming through the window shades. After making her morning declarations and spending time with God, she opened the shades to see another beautiful day in East Texas. The sun was shining through the tall pine trees, and one of her favorite things was to see the birds come to the bird feeders that Monroe had strategically placed right outside her window. As she made herself comfortable in her recliner, she picked up her journal and opened it to the next blank page with this written at the top:

Describe the Greatest Summer Day

As she picked up her pen, she thought, "That's easy because this is the Greatest Summer Day."

"The Greatest summer day is one where the sun is shining brightly… like today. The birds are singing… like today."

She closed her eyes and took a deep breath from her oxygen tank. She continued, "The Greatest summer day is when a cool breeze is blowing through the tops of the trees. The butterflies painted with many colors are getting nectar from the many, different kinds of flowers. A long walk down the road, without the need for oxygen... smelling every tree and flower. Breathing deeply... easily, and filling my lungs with God's fresh air. Walking as long and as far and as fast as I want to, never getting tired or needing any kind of assistance. The Greatest Summer Day for me is to bask in the goodness of God, enjoying every part of all the things He has created just for me.

The Greatest Summer Day for me is found in Frances of Assisi's prayer:

'Lord, make me an instrument of your peace. Where there is hatred, let me bring your love; where there is injury, let me bring mercy; where there is doubt, let me bring faith; where there is darkness, let me bring light; and where there is sadness, let me bring your joy.

O divine Master, grant that I may not so much seek to be consoled as to console; to be understood as to understand; to be loved as to love with all my soul.

For it is in giving that we receive; it is in pardoning that we are pardoned; and it is in dying that we are born to eternal life.'"

Chapter 19

The Greatest Recipe

As she glanced to the next page of her journal, Mamaw saw:

What is your Greatest Recipe?

She wrote the following in her journal dated July 11, 1999:

"There are so many things I like, but only a few things I love. I like all kinds of foods, but I love desserts. When I think about recipes for food, I am reminded that The Greatest Recipe should be the one you have for your life. So, I will write my thoughts about how to have a Greatest Recipe for life and relate it to my Greatest Recipe for food.

First, you have to know what you want. I have discovered that most people get more in life of what they don't want than what they do want because they never decide what it IS they want.

I love to cook for my family, but the more people there are in the room, it seems the less most people know what it is that they want to eat. I'll ask the family, 'What would everyone like to eat?' and most of the time, the answer is, it doesn't matter, or they are not particular. I have always been passionate about food and that seems to correlate with my life.

93

Second, once you know what you love and want, you have to get a picture in your head of what it looks like. Before you ever cook something, you have to have a picture of what it is going to look like.

Third, you have to gather the ingredients. You have to put a plan together for what you are going to create, and it is important to lay it all out. That's really what a recipe is… a plan on paper. You write out exactly what you need in specific detail based on the picture you have in your mind of what it will look like in the end.

Fourth, you have to have the right ingredients added at the right time. You have to know when to do what. And you measure the ingredients out and add them in proper order.

Fifth, you have a start time and a finish time. And you inspect what you expect the outcome to be, all during the process. It just makes sense that everything you decide to make has its own process. There is no progress, without a process.

Finally, you serve it in the right dish at the right time. There is always a right dish to serve with and there is always a right time to serve what you have so excellently prepared.

Again, I have discovered these truths about recipes to be the same for life as for food. With that said, let me share my Greatest Dessert Recipe, because that is what I am most passionate about."

Soft Gingerbread

1 cup of molasses
2 teaspoons of soda (level)
½ cup of shortening or butter
1 cup of boiling water
½ cup of sugar
2 well beaten eggs
2 ½ cups of flour
1 teaspoon allspice
1 teaspoon of cinnamon

Directions:
- Mix sugar, Molasses and shortening/butter with ½ cup of boiling water
- Then, add flour, all spice, and cinnamon
- Dissolve soda in the other ½ cup of water
- Add well beaten eggs last

Bake in 9 X 11 loaf pan in oven at 350 degrees for about 40 minutes.

Tenet # 17

Most people get more of what they
don't want in life, rather than what they
want, because they never decide what
it is that they do want. Decide what you
want and make a Great Recipe.

Chapter 20

The Greatest Times

Over the next several months Mamaw struggled with her health. She was no longer able to breath without the assistance of oxygen. Her lungs had been irreparably damaged due to the experimental laser surgery and treatment for her breast cancer. As difficult as the last few years of her life had been, she felt very blessed to be living with her daughter Gayle and son-in-love Monroe. These times with her children were her Greatest Times.

Gayle and Monroe's house was nestled on 26 wooded acres with hundreds of beautiful towering Pine trees divinely scattered throughout the property. The one lane road that led to their house was reminiscent of a painting by Claude Oscar Monet called *The Avenue*. This was the place, with its lush landscapes, where Mamaw would spend the last five years of her life, and the last days of her life.

She not only had her daughter, Gayle, who she lived with, but also Gayle's sister, Ann, and her husband had built a wing onto Gayle and Monroe's house. In fact, all of Mamaw's children had retired to this most beautiful part of Texas. Her oldest son, Ernest and his wife had 20 acres. Her youngest son David had 20 acres. All of their properties were adjoined by a pond. Not just any pond, but a pond very much like Henry David Thoreau described in his book, *Walden; Life in the Woods.*

"I went to the woods because I wished to live deliberately, to front only essential facts of life, and see if I could learn what it had to teach, and not, when I came to die, discover that I had not lived. I did not wish to live what was not life, living is so dear; nor did I wish to practice resignation, unless it was quite necessary. I wanted to live deep and suck all the marrow of life...."

Thoreau spent two years of his life beside the still waters of Walden's Pond. As he describes it, the pond became a place of vast transformation of the face of the world and restoration of the full powers of the soul. A place where Mamaw could, as Thoreau said, "meet our lives and live fully."

In the latter years of her life, Mamaw lived some of her heaven on earth by getting to spend time with her children every day. At least once a week most of the family would gather at Gayle and Monroe's house to eat and enjoy the company of one another, and especially, to be in the presence of Mamaw.

It was November 25, 1999, Thanksgiving Day. The family had gathered together at Gayle and Monroe's house for a Thanksgiving meal. As a family tradition, all four children, Ernest, Gayle, Ann, and David would gather with their spouses and watch the Dallas Cowboys play their annual Thanksgiving Day game before they ate. These were some of Mamaw's Greatest Times because she had all her children, all together

Mamaw's Tenets for Life

in the same place. And what made a good time, a Great Time, was when the Cowboys would win on Thanksgiving Day.

The Dallas Cowboys were America's Team. In fact, there had only been two seasons since 1966 that the Cowboys had not played on Thanksgiving Day. In 1975 and 1977, the NFL, in response to complaints from other teams that Dallas' annual home Thanksgiving game was unfair, gave the slots to other teams. The television ratings were so low that the NFL gave the Thanksgiving Day game back to Dallas and they have played host to a game on the fourth Thursday in November every year since 1978.

Living up to their name as "America's Team," the Dallas Cowboys beat the Miami Dolphins 20 to 0. All the family gathered around the table and Mamaw, said, "Before we pray, I just want to tell you all how much I love you. Today has been so special to me because I got to spend it with you." She continued, "A few months ago, Allen gave me a journal to write about my life, my memories, my good times and my bad times, my best things and my worst things... he just wanted me to record some things about my life for all of you, my family. So, after we pray and while we eat, I would like to read to each of you a favorite story I have about you... if that's ok?"

"Of course, Mother," David said, "we would all love that."

No one at the table realized this would be Mamaw's last Thanksgiving Day with them. But something inside her heart knew it would be.

As everyone began to eat their turkey and dressing, Mamaw opened her journal and said with a loving smile,

The Greatest Times

"This is the Greatest Time I have ever had. Thank you all for making my life so great. I love you with all of my heart."

Chapter 21

The Greatest December

I t was a crisp December morning, as Gayle entered Mamaw's room and said, "Good morning, Mother. Would you like to have a cup of coffee with me?"

"Oh honey, I would love that. Maybe we could have our morning devotional together," Mamaw suggested. As Mamaw walked slowly towards the kitchen, she asked, "Gayle do you know what the temperature is outside? It looks like such a beautiful day and if it's not too cold, later on I would like to sit on the porch for a little bit."

"It's actually a very nice day Mother. It's crisp outside, but not cold," Gayle replied.

Mamaw walked over to the window and looked outside. Her look turned into a stare as she thought about one December almost 70 years before.

Gayle put her arm around Mamaw as she handed her coffee. "Mother I saw you over here just starring out the window while I was making your coffee. What 'ya thinking about?"

"Well..." Mamaw paused. "I was thinking about your daddy."

Gayle was silent. That was the last thing she ever expected to hear. Mamaw turned from the big bay window and sat down at the dining room table. Gayle took a seat across from her, and as she took a sip of her coffee, she said, "Can you tell me about it? Why were you thinking about daddy?"

"Well baby, in two days, it would be our 68th wedding anniversary."

"Wow…" Gayle said slowly.

"Yes, it was on December 20, 1931, that your daddy and I got married. It was the Greatest December I ever remember," Mamaw said with a grateful smile. "I was just thinking… I was just remembering the good times. I've never stopped loving him. I learned something, sweetie, and that is when you choose to be your best for God, He gives you the power to see the best in other people, even when the worst has been displayed."

"Mother, that's not only why I respect you so much, but that's one of the reasons I love you so much. You have lived striving to be your best for God, and for all these years I have had a front row seat to observe your life. You really have always… always seen the best in other people. And it seems to me, that more times than not, it has been when their worst has been displayed," Gayle said.

"That's the test baby. Can you see the best when the worst has been displayed?" Mamaw explained. "It's a choice that only we can make. It's a choice to see people the way God sees them. It's a choice to see people the way you would like for people to see you. It's a choice to believe that God is working all things together for your good… the good and the bad things. It's a choice to believe that God has got the whole world in His hands, like the old song says," Mamaw said with a smile.

"'He's got the whole world, in His hands," Mamaw began to sing lightly, "He's got the whole world, in His hands. He's got the whole world in His hands, He's got the whole world in His hands.'"

"That's why you have always heard me say, 'God's got this! He always has and He always will!'" Mamaw reached over and grabbed her favorite devotional book, "*My Utmost for His Highest*" by Oswald Chambers. She turned to December 18 and read the title:

The Test of Loyalty

"Well isn't that interesting Mother?" Gayle asked.

"Listen to what the scripture is for the day, Gayle," Mamaw said. "'*And we know that all things work together for good for them that love God. Romans 8:28*'"

Mamaw continued to read, "'*The test of loyalty is if we learn to worship God in trying circumstances....*'"

"That's good," said Gayle.

"And…" Mamaw continued, "time is a test, because we determine over time, not just who we are or what someone did to us, but the way we live our lives proves or disproves who He is in our lives."

"December 1931 used to be my Greatest December, but that has changed. Sixty-eight years later I can say that THIS is my Greatest December because every day, I GET TO be with you, my precious daughter." With that Mamaw got up and gave Gayle the warmest hug she had ever received.

"Yes, Mother, I feel the same way. God is so good to allow me to be with you… in your presence, every day."

"Thank you honey. I'm going to go get my journal and go sit outside for a bit. I love you baby."

"I love you too, Mother, very much."

Tenet #18

When you choose to be the BEST you can BE, you will SEE the BEST in others.

Chapter 22

The Greatest Tragedy

Mamaw grabbed her favorite quilt she had stitched over 30 years ago and sat down in a chair on the front porch. She closed her eyes as the cool breeze hit her face. In the silence of the moment, she listened as the wind blew the leaves across the front lawn. She could hear the birds singing. She thought, "So good to know God is in command and He made this day just for me... thank You God," she said out loud.

As she picked up her journal, she opened to the next blank page and she read:

Describe your Greatest Tragedy and how it affected your life

Mamaw sighed and began to write:

"I suppose it was the night in the Spring of 1961, when a man handed me a paper. It was a paper that said my husband had filed for divorce. I knew he hadn't been the husband, loving and caring and all, that he had been through the years, but... I was in a state of shock and couldn't believe my marriage was over. I still loved him, with all his faults and failures."

Mamaw paused as tears begin to flow from her eyes. She had pushed her small portable oxygen tank outside because she needed it to breath. But in that moment, she pulled the nose piece that delivered the oxygen from her nostrils, and reached under her quilt into her robe and grabbed a tissue. As she raised her glasses to wipe her eyes, she took a long, deep breath.

For the first time in a long time she smelled the fresh cool December air. It seemed as though she could feel her lungs take in the fresh air uninhibitedly. "I think I'll just breath on my own for a while," she thought, and then she continued writing:

"It felt like a bad dream. Then, I began to cry." As she wrote, tears began to fill her eyes again. "I walked the floor back and forth, for how long I don't know. Then, I went outside. I paced up and down our sidewalk. The sobs came from the bottom of my stomach. I walked back into that big house of ours and felt more alone than I have ever felt. All four of our children were married.

I called my oldest son, Ernest, and he said, 'I'm coming over immediately Mother, and you are coming to my house.' I didn't stay for too long. All the kids came over and surrounded me, along with a host of friends and my pastor. I will never forget how sweet they were, in my darkest hour.

The divorce was final on June 6, 1961. After thirty years of marriage I had to begin again. I had to start over. I had to get a job. I had to support myself.

And thank God, I still had hope...."

Mamaw heard a car coming toward the house, and as she

wiped the remaining tears from her eyes she could see Allen pulling up to the front of the house.

"Hey Mamaw! I came to see you!" he said as he walked up the front steps of the porch.

"Awe baby, I'm so glad to see you!" Mamaw said.

"What are you doing out here? It's getting cold. Why don't you have your oxygen on, Mamaw?"

"Well honey, I've been writing in the journal you gave me, and it was such a beautiful day that I decided to take off my oxygen and enjoy me some fresh air! It has been so nice. Are you hungry? Come on inside and let's get some food. You want some iced tea?" Mamaw asked with a smile in her voice.

"Yes ma'am."

Allen helped Mamaw get into the house, and Mamaw said, "Ok, I am going to fix you your favorite meal Allen," as she reached up and clasped his nose with two fingers.

"I can't wait," Allen exclaimed. "Meatloaf, scalloped potatoes, fried okra, pinto beans and corn bread," Mamaw said. "Sit down and visit with your Mother, and I will get everything ready."

Allen didn't know it, but this would be the last time Mamaw would ever cook his favorite meal.

Chapter 23

The Greatest Memory

"That was AMAZING Mamaw!" Allen exclaimed. "My favorite meal forever and for always!"

"Thank you honey. I'm glad you enjoyed it. I haven't cooked in a very long time, but I wanted to do that for you," Mamaw said.

"Thank you... thank you. Ok, Mom, Dad, I want us all to go into the den. I have a very exciting announcement," Allen said.

"What is it?" his mother asked.

"That's what I came over to talk to you guys about. So, come in here so I can tell you," Allen said.

Gayle and Mamaw came into the den from the kitchen and sat down on the blue velour sectional coach. "Ok, are you guys ready?" Allen said with anticipation.

"Yes, tell us! What is it Allen?" Gayle asked.

"Mom, Dad... Mamaw, I am starting a church," Allen said.

"What?" Allen's mother asked. "You are starting a church? Where?"

"Yes, where?" Mamaw asked.

"In Frisco, Texas!" For the next hour, Allen gave all the

details about the new church he would be starting.

Mamaw listened intently and then asked, "Is that in Collin County?"

"I think so," Allen answered.

Mamaw got up from the couch and went to her bed room to get her journal. As she came back into the den, she still was not wearing her oxygen and she seemed to have a skip in her step.

"Do you remember your Great-Aunt Ruby?" Mamaw asked.

"Yes. I loved her and Uncle Jack. I loved how Uncle Jack played the guitar and sang. Mamaw do you remember that time when I was a youth pastor and I had Uncle Jack come and sing and preach to my youth group?" Allen asked.

"Yes, Yes! He loved that!" Mamaw said.

"And all the kids loved him! He was like 100 years old or something!" Allen said laughing. "That will go down as one of my all-time greatest memories."

"Well, let me tell you about my Greatest Memory," Mamaw said. "You asked me about it in the journal, so I will just read to you what I wrote. What you may not know, is Jack Kitchens was Aunt Ruby's second husband."

Allen interrupted, "Her second husband Mamaw? No! I didn't know that."

"Her first husband passed away. His name was Mansel McKinney. Let me read from my journal." Mamaw began to read:

"My Greatest Memory happened around 1932. My husband and I hadn't been married that long. He was going from job to job trying to 'make ends meet.' No one knew we were on the front of what would become known as the Great Depression. There were lines everywhere. People lined up to get a job. People stood in lines for food. It was a very difficult time.

It was during that time that my husband and I lived with my sister Ruby and her husband Mansel McKinney. The city of McKinney, Texas was named after Mansel's family. We all lived in what was called the 'McKinney House.'"

Mamaw continued to read;

"One night I had a vision. It was a real vision from God. I looked outside and could see a ladder going up into the heavens. In my vision, I remembered the story of Jacobs ladder, and the story in Genesis 28, where he had the same kind of dream. I remember that Jacob saw a *'ladder like this set up on the earth and it's top reached the heavens'* like in my dream. I remember thinking, this is so real.

In Jacob's dream, he saw 'angels ascending and descending' on the ladder. In my dream, I saw all my family members going up, 11 of them and I was last. As years passed, each one of those 10 people died and went to heaven in the order that I saw in the dream. I am the only one left.

In Jacobs dream, *'the Lord stood above the ladder and said, I am the Lord God of Abraham your father and God of Isaac; the land on which you lie I will give to you and your descendants.'* God told Jacob that his descendants shall spread abroad and in you and in your seed all the families of the earth shall be blessed. He told him that He would keep him wherever he went and that He would bring him back to the land. Then, Jacob wakes up and says, *'How awesome is this place! This is none other than the house of God and this is the gate of heaven.'*

In this vision, God spoke to me about my family generationally, that they would all go to heaven, and they have. But why did I see it here, in McKinney, at the McKinney House? This was the most vivid vision I had ever had. It is my Greatest Memory of God showing me something, and yet, I know it is only in part because I only know what I know, and I do not know what I don't know.

So, maybe my Greatest Memory is God speaking to me, not just about past generations who have gone before me to heaven, but maybe God is speaking to me like He was to Jacob about my future generations that will bring heaven to earth?"

As she looked up at Allen, she said, "Do you remember what the place was called that Jacob had this dream?"

Allen said, "Yes, it was Bethel."

"Do you remember the name of the church you were raised in?" Mamaw asked with a smile.

"Yes, it was called Bethel."

She then said, "And you are starting a church in the county that I had the vision in...."

Everyone in the room paused and pondered. Allen was hearing this vison for the first time from Mamaw, and his question in the journal had provoked her to share it, or it may have never been known.

"Maybe God is bringing my descendants back to this land. Maybe the vision was not just meant to be a Great Memory, but maybe it was a picture of the Great Future that God is going to bring about through our family in Collin County" Mamaw said with a reverence in her voice.

"When is this going to happen honey?" Allen's mom asked.

"Do ya'll remember when I was 37, that a pastor friend of mine asked me, 'Do you think you will ever pastor a church?'"

"Yes, I remember that," Gayle answered.

"And what I told that pastor friend of mine is that I would answer that question when I was forty. So, Mom, Dad... Mamaw, I am going to start the church on my 40th birthday, January 9, 2000!"

"We are so proud of you," Monroe said.

"Yes, we are" Mamaw and Gayle chimed in.

Chapter 24

The Greatest Miracle

Mamaw and Allen had always been close. The truth is, that everyone who had the privilege of being in Mamaw's presence felt like they were her favorite person in the whole world. But the bond that Allen and Mamaw had was special. She was a part of his Greatest Miracle.

It was December 31, 1999. All the family had come over for New Year's Eve. It had been a lovely evening and it truly was an exclamation point to a wonderful year. Mamaw was the first to say goodnight. She wanted to finish the journal before the end of the year, but didn't quit make it. Tonight, she would do what she could.

As Mamaw opened her journal, she felt tired, and yet there were still a few questions Allen had asked for her to answer in her journal. She knew she wanted to answer one of the last two questions;

What is the Greatest Miracle you have ever seen?

With a shaky hand, Mamaw begin to write:

"Gayle, my daughter, was going to be attending a church choir banquet and she ask me to babysit Ray and Allen. Cindy hadn't been born yet. When I arrived, Gayle told me that she had just put Allen down for a nap and to check on him in about 30 or 45 minutes. I had been cleaning in the kitchen when Ray, who was two at the time, said, 'Mamaw, Mamaw, Allen is all blue.' I didn't pay much attention to it, but a few minutes later, when Ray came in the second time, I thought I'd better check on Allen because maybe Ray had done something to him.

When I walked into the bedroom where Gayle had left Allen for a nap, I saw his play pen next to the bed, and at first, I did not notice anything out of the ordinary. The closer I got to the baby pen, I realized something was very wrong. Allen was completely wrapped inside a plastic dry-cleaning bag.

I felt like my heart was going to pop out of my chest. I reached down immediately to pick him up and noticed that there was a lot of blood. Somehow, he had become entangled in a plastic clothes bag and he was not breathing. Blood was coming from his ears, nose, and mouth. It looked like it was coming from everywhere. I raced to the phone praying and crying, and I called the emergency number.

An ambulance was dispatched. Allen was not breathing. Five minutes passed... fifteen minutes passed. I was frantically praying as I waited for an ambulance that seemed to be never coming. I went outside and stood on the corner, holding Allen in my arms, blood pouring from his body onto me. He was not breathing. He hadn't been breathing. Where was the ambulance? I prayed and prayed and cried and believed. No one came.

Mamaw's Tenets for Life

After what seemed like an eternity, a firetruck with its emergency lights and siren on, rushed down our street. A man by the name of E. R. Coffman said, 'I am so sorry! The ambulance had a flat tire. We intercepted the call and came as fast as we could. How long has he been like this?' he asked as they began to work on Allen.

I told him I was not sure, but I knew I had been standing on that curb for at least 30 minutes, and I didn't know how long it was before that. They tried everything: Mouth to Mouth resuscitation and everything else they knew to do. And then it was over. They pronounced Allen dead on the scene.

1961 was my most difficult year. My husband of 30 years was gone, and I never felt more helpless and alone than I did that day on that curb holding my lifeless grandson. I did the only thing I knew to do. I looked up and cried out to God and said, 'Father God! The same Spirit that raised Jesus Christ from the dead dwells inside this baby boy. Jesus, You conquered death, hell, and the grave and I ask you to resurrect this boy!'

I shouted it! I didn't care who heard me! I didn't care if those firemen thought I was crazy! And I had no sooner prayed that prayer when the sheet they had covered him with blew off, his eyes popped open, and he came back to life! It was the Greatest Miracle I had ever seen!

Since then I have realized that out of your greatest tragedies can come your greatest miracles!"

As Mamaw closed the journal, she moved from her chair to her bed. "Thank You, Lord, for another year to bring You

The Greatest Miracle

glory and honor."

She went on to do what she always did every night before she went to sleep. She thanked God for His wisdom, knowledge, and understanding. She thanked Him for His divine favor on her life. And as she closed her eyes, she prayed for every member of her family to come to a saving knowledge of Jesus Christ. And like always, Mamaw feel asleep praying.

The story of my coming back to life was recorded on the front page of the Dallas Morning News Thanksgiving Day 1961

Tenet #19

Out of your Greatest Tragedies can come your Greatest Miracles.

Chapter 25

The Greatest Legacy

On January 9, 2000 Allen launched his church in Frisco, Texas. It was a great opening celebration with over 700 people in attendance. Several local mayors were there along with other city officials. But for Allen, there was only one VIP that mattered most, and that was Mamaw. Unfortunately, she was not able to attend. Her health had deteriorated to the point that she could not leave the house.

The service was held on a Sunday night, so Allen had to wait until the next day to go see Mamaw. He wanted everything to be perfect, so he had his video team putting together a professionally edited video just for Mamaw.

On January 10, 2000 Allen drove to East Texas to see his Mamaw. He had talked to his mother Gayle and knew that Mamaw was very sick. As he drove the two-hour drive, his mind was filled with vivid memories of the special times he and Mamaw had shared. All the Malibu Adventures from childhood. All the incredible meals they had shared. He reminisced about the many Life Lessons she had taught him. He cried as he recounted her battle with cancer and the years she had struggled physically, and yet, she never complained.

He thought about how he never knew his grandfather except through her expressions of love for him. The fact that she never spoke a negative word about him or anyone… ever. With tears streaming down his face, he remembered all the times she prayed for him. He thought of all her special ways with him. The special names she called him that nobody else did. He thought about her special touch… that thing that only she did, when she would clasp his nose gently between her fingers. His most fond and deep hearted memories were of their times at the altar… at Bethel. That place that Jacob called "the gateway of heaven."

As he pulled up to the house, he couldn't wait to tell Mamaw about the service. His only regret is that the video of the service would not be ready until Tuesday, January 11.

Mamaw was happy to see Allen. Her mood was up but Allen could tell she wasn't doing well. They spent hours together. All day and into the night they talked, ate, and watched movies together.

On Tuesday, the video was hand delivered. Mamaw and Allen sat down together in her room so she could be in her recliner. Gayle had made them some soup, and Allen had crackers and butter with his favorite iced tea.

"Honey before we watch your first church service, I just want to tell you that I finished your journal you gave me," Mamaw said with a smile.

"Oh, Mamaw, I am so glad," Allen said.

"I am too baby. I hope it is what you want. I did my best to complete it, and there is some pretty personal stuff in there," she said with a sweet smile.

"Well, let's maybe look at it together later, Mamaw, but right now, I want to show you the service. I'm so excited!"

Allen turned down the lights and the VHS video began to play. Mamaw's face was beaming. As they watched the service together, Mamaw rubbed Allen's arm softly. She held his hand and gently squeezed it while she did. She reached over and rubbed his nose and said, "This is so good honey. I am loving this."

She loved the worship team, and after she listened to Allen's message she said, "That was the greatest message I have ever heard sweetie."

"Thank you, Mamaw. You don't have to say that," Allen said.

"I know baby. I don't have to say it, but it's true. I wrote in the journal, when you ask me who my favorite preachers are, that out of all of them—Billy Graham, Oral Roberts—you Allen, are my favorite, and not just because you are my grandson. I talk about it in the journal. You bring the Word of God alive to me in a way I've never heard it."

"Mamaw, you are going to make me cry. You know what I am doing? I am just preaching back to you what you have taught me and many others your whole life. How many people in the history of the world can say they taught Sunday School in the same church for 50 years? Wow! That still blows me away Mamaw, and I got to be your student. I got to be your follower as you followed Christ. I got to live with you and be the beneficiary of your greatness, Mamaw. I am a part of your legacy, the legacy that you have lived."

"Awe baby, I don't know about that, but what I do know,

is I am so proud of you," Mamaw humbly expressed. "God brought you back to life, Allen, for a purpose: His purpose. And I get to see it full circle. 40 years later, in Collin County, there's a ladder and there's a Bethel, the house of God, and how awesome is that place, and this place with you right now...."

Mamaw laid her head back and said, "God is so good. I love you Allen with all of my heart."

"I love you, Mamaw, and I am so excited you got to see our first service."

"Me too, baby, me too," Mamaw said. "Take this journal honey."

Allen and Mamaw prayed together and hugged and kissed and said goodbye ... for the last time.

The next day, on January 12, Monroe knocked on Mamaw's door. It was 8:00 am. There was no answer because Mamaw woke up one day before her 88th birthday in heaven.

What is interesting is that Mamaw had many visions from God throughout her life, but one of the last visions she had was that she was in heaven and there were a bunch of gifts that were wrapped.

She asked the Lord in the vision, "What are these?"

He said, "They are gifts for you." And she woke up.

Now she knows what that vision means.

On the last page of Mamaw's journal was this question:

What advice about life do you want others to remember?

Mamaw wrote:

- Live each day as if it was your last.
- Be sensitive to the Holy Spirit so you will listen when He speaks to you.
- Be kind even when someone hurts you.
- Forgive and forget the bad things.
- Be thoughtful and considerate.
- Try to help others to be happy no matter what they face.
- Trust our Heavenly Father to take care of you. He will never leave you.
- Try to do a good deed each day.
- Encourage someone today.
- Do not murmur or complain.

Elevate Life Church
The Cathedral of Frisco"

The Greatest Legacy

Tenet #20

Live the legacy that you want to leave.

A Final Word

Much of this parable is true. Mamaw was my Mamaw. I am Allen. Ray and Cindy in the story are actually my brother and sister. Gayle and Monroe are my mom and dad. When I refer to Mamaw's journal, this book contains actual excerpts from the journal that I gave her. The last entry is word for word.

My purpose in giving her the journal was to carry her legacy in our family, never knowing I would share it with the world.

Mamaw was and is my hero. She lived everything I have written in this book, and more. She did indeed live the legacy that she wanted to leave. I am forever the grateful beneficiary of her greatness. So are my wife and my children, and now, my children's children. My family of choice, Elevate Life Church, is the beneficiaries of Mamaw's indelible legacy.

I did not know when I was looking for the woman that I would marry, that I would know so quickly and so early in my life who that Precious person was.

At 15, I met Sheila Wood. I knew from the moment I met her and talked with her that she carried the same type of

Precious spirit that my Mamaw had. When I ask her to be my girlfriend on January 20, 1976, I told her after she said "Yes!" that I would celebrate her on the 20th for as long as we were together. As of the writing of this book, I have celebrated her on the 20th of every month for over 40 years.

You may think that is weird, or you may admire it. I did it to honor the YES on that day and will continue to do that for the rest of my life with her.

Why is that significant?

Because when you honor God, my Mamaw taught me that He will honor you. That's a bonus "tenet."

My first grandbaby was born on January 20. It was a Tuesday, 40 years later, on the exact day of the week Sheila said, Yes!

My second grandbaby was born on September 20.

I introduced my brother, who's middle name is Ray (Ray in the story), to his wife, who is my wife's older sister. Their first 2 grandbabies were born on the 20th.

My wife's twin sister is married to a guy that I introduced her to. Their first grandbaby was born on the 20th.

One could think this all is a coincidence, or somehow, we all planned this. But I believe because I honored the 20th, that anything I am a part of is somehow imprinted with what I chose to honor.

What does this have to do with my Mamaw?

Her wedding day was December 20, 1931. I did not know that until I thoroughly read her journal as research for this book.

According to Daniel in the bible, "God is indeed the Wonderful Numberer."

I hope you enjoyed the story, but more importantly, I hope you were inspired by my Mamaw's life and the "tenets" she taught me to live by.

I can only hope that God will continue to bless me, not just to carry her message to the world, but so I can live the legacy that she lived every day ahead of me. And even if I touch just one, maybe that will be one that God puts His hand on to impact millions... for the glory of God.

If there is one thing I know, God knows our lives from beginning to end, and we don't. Mamaw taught me that God is faithful, and we just need to be faithful in doing our part. Thank you Mamaw.

"Yet God has made everything beautiful for its own time. He had planted eternity in the human heart, but even so, people cannot see the whole scope of God's work from beginning to end."

Ecclesiastes 3:11

God bless you,
Keith

Mamaw's Tenets

Tenet #1
God's got us. He always has and He always will, and for that, we will always be thankful.

Tenet #2
Every day we live is a GET TO, not a HAVE TO.

Tenet #3
The most important people are the ones who put others before themselves, and in doing so, you are serving their best interests above your own.

Tenet #4
You cannot dictate everything that happens TO you, but you can dictate what happens IN you.

Tenet #5
By choosing to Wake up and MAKE UP your bed, you're learning to wake up to what you can make GO UP in your life.

Tenet #6
You get second things only by putting first things first.

Tenet #7
What you take care of, will eventually take care of you.

Tenet #8
Everybody has enough of a leash to succeed or fail, to do right or to do wrong, to help themselves or hang themselves.

Tenet #9
When you are grateful, your life will be GREAT-FULL.

Tenet #10
You cannot control what other people do to you, but you can control what you do to others.

Tenet #11
God is faithful.

Tenet #12
Seize the Moment and always take a picture.

Tenet #13
Where you are from is not who you are.

Tenet #14
If you don't have something good to say, don't say it.

Tenet #15
When you have a favorite verse, it will lead to a favored life.

Tenet #16
Your life lessons are your life lessons. If you learn them well, everyone around you will benefit.

Tenet # 17
Most people get more of what they don't want in life, rather than what they want, because they never decide what it is that they do want. Decide what you want and make a Great Recipe.

Tenet #18
When you choose to be the BEST you can BE, you will SEE the BEST in others.

Tenet #19
Out of your Greatest Tragedies can come your Greatest Miracles.

Tenet #20
Live the legacy that you want to leave.

Bonus Tenet
When you honor God, He will honor you.

A Final Word

This is a picture of my Mamaw and father (James "Monroe"). My mother and father were headed to church one Sunday morning in 1990 and stopped on the side of the side of the road to take this picture. The bluebonnet is the Texas State Flower, and in the Spring they grow wild all along the Texas highways.

None of us knew that Mamaw and my father would be the first two in our family to go to heaven. I can only imagine that they are standing in heaven together surrounded by bluebonnets just like these.

When I was a child, my father took me for rides in his cars and trucks. My most memorable ride was in the '69 Cuda as recorded in this book.

Our last ride together before he passed away, was on my Harley Trike in Florida. It didn't matter where we went, it just mattered that we were together.

I always remember, he would say to me, "Come ride with me, Keith." I would say, "Where are we going?" He would reply, "That doesn't matter. I just want to be with you."

Thank you, dad, for just wanting to be with me. I look forward to riding together in heaven.

Other Books by Keith A. Craft

Within the pages of his motivational and inspirational self-help book, *Your Divine Fingerprint: The Force That Makes You Unstoppable*, are the tools to help you discover a unique fingerprint that you have been given. These tools will help you deploy your unique difference that your family needs, your marriage needs, your job needs, your faith needs—that the world needs. And when you embrace and live in that uniqueness, you celebrate the glory of God.

Leadershipology 101: Quotes to Live By are inspirational quotes to propel you in your leadership quest. Keith has put together his collection of leadership quotes and has included a "Keith Craft's Thought Behind the Quote" to provide an additional thought to both challenge and inspire. *Leadershipology 101: Quotes to Live By* is an excellent resource of short, life-changing quotes which have given life to people worldwide.

Aaron and Miriam, the brother and sister of Moses, fell prey to the ultimate scheme of Satan and unleashed a horrible spirit in the camp of the children of Israel. Yes, the devil has specific plans and you need to be totally aware of what they are. Even more, he has a weapon designed to keep you from having a right relationship with God. His objective is to strike at the very purpose of your life. With *How to Defeat Satan's Number One Weapon*, you will be equipped to win your personal battle with the Evil One.

76714602R00088

Made in the USA
Columbia, SC
27 September 2019